ORCHARD BOOKS

338 Euston Road, London NW1 3BH

Orchard Books Australia

Level 17/207 Kent Street, Sydney, NSW 2000

First published in hardback in Great Britain in 2009 by Orchard Books

First published in paperback in 2010

ISBN 978 1 84616 752 2 (hardback)

ISBN 978 1 40830 776 2 (paperback)

A CIP catalogue record for this book is available from the British Library.

1 3 5 7 9 10 8 6 4 2 (hardback)

1 3 5 7 9 10 8 6 4 2 (paperback)

Printed in Great Britain

Orchard Books is a division of Hachette Children's Books,
an Hachette UK company.

www.hachette.co.uk

JACK-in-the-BOX?
AND
TALL-TALE JACK

MICHAEL
LAWRENCE

TONY
ROSS

ORCHARD BOOKS

JACK-in-the-BOX?

He was found in a box on the orphanage steps. He was a baby at the time. On the side of the box were the words THIS WAY UP. As a temporary measure until they decided on a more suitable name, the people who ran the orphanage called him after the box.

But the temporary measure stuck, and years later they were still saying,

'Eat your porridge,

　　This-Way-Up,'

or 'Sweep the floor,

　　This-Way-Up. Earn your keep

or it's back to the steps for you.'

For a long time the boy thought nothing of his unusual name. As the only one he'd ever known, This-Way-Up seemed as natural to him as Joseph does to a Joseph, Henry to a Henry, and anything you like to a dog. But in his eleventh or twelfth year the other boys began to find something funny in his name and smirk behind their hands, and This-Way-Up wondered why. He went to see the head of the orphanage to ask where his name had come from. Put on the spot, the head told him.

'So This-Way-Up isn't really a name?' the boy said, shocked to learn that it had come off the box he'd been delivered in.

'It could be worse,' the head said.

'It could?' said This-Way-Up.

'Certainly. If you'd come in a different box I might be sitting here talking to Pineapple Chunks, Fresh Fish or Handle-With-Care.'

This-Way-Up was not consoled.

'I want a name. A real name.'

'You can borrow mine,' the head offered magnanimously.

'What's yours?'

'Ethelbert.'

'I'd rather sew my mouth up with chicken wire,' said This-Way-Up.

'Ingrate,' said the head, and put him out in the street.

In the big wide wonderful world for the first time since he'd been packed into his box as a squalling brat, This-Way-Up decided to find a proper name for himself. The trouble was, the only names he knew were the half-dozen allocated to the fifty-three other boys at the orphanage, each of which had a number attached,

like Brian 4,

Struwelpeter 7,

and so on.

He didn't want one of those; he wanted one without a number. He walked away from the orphanage pondering how to find out what names were available.

Near the orphanage were some woods. At the edge of the woods he saw a notice with an arrow pointing into them. On the arrow were some words.

This-Way-Up followed the arrow until he came to a cottage. The cottage was covered in ivy, with roses round the door, and would have been very attractive if it hadn't been a ruin. Next to the ruined cottage stood a shed. On the shed door was another notice.

This-Way-Up knocked.

'Who's that knocking on my door?' said
an irritated voice.

'I'm looking for the
Wise Old Crone of the Woods,'
he answered.

The door creaked open. An ancient biddy
with a hooked nose and a shawl looked out.

'You've found her. What do you want?'

'I need a name. I don't have one, you see.
Not a proper one. I thought you might have a
few suggestions, being wise and all.'

'I know about potions and lotions,' said the crone. 'I can predict your future, tell you what the weather's going to do, teach you to say Llanfairpwllgwyngyllgogerychwyrndrobwllllantysiliogogogoch without a stutter. But names? Sorry, not my scene.'

She shut the door.

This-Way-Up turned away.

The door flew open again.

'Wait! I've just thought of a name for you!'

His eyes brightened. 'Really?'

'Humphrey,' she said.

His eyes dulled.

'Or Huw,' said the crone. 'You could do worse than Huw. You know who's who with a Huw, or even a Hugh.

And what about Nathaniel?

Or Digby?

Or Roderick,

Seth,

Septimus,

Orlando,

Bartholomew?

What about Ted?'

While This-Way-Up was deciding that he didn't care for any of these, the Wise Old Crone of the Woods shut the door again.

He turned away.

The shed door flew open.

'One more.'

'Yes?' he said hopefully.

'Jack.'

The door slammed.

This-Way-Up waited but the door didn't open again. As he turned to go once more, he glimpsed a wood spirit flitting from tree to tree in a diaphanous green dress with leaves in her hair.

'Dryad!' he cried, dashing after her.
'Dryad, wait, I need your help!'

The dryad paused. Her hooded eyes cast a shaft of dusty sunlight across him. 'Why should I help you? Your kind cut down trees and make their spirits homeless. My own fine sycamore was felled last month and I've been without bark or bole ever since.'

'I've never cut down a tree,' This-Way-Up assured her. 'I've been in an orphanage all my life and know nothing of the world. I don't even have a name.'

'Then we have something in common,' the spirit said with an inkling of interest. 'For I too am nameless.'

'You are? Why? Weren't you given one either?'

'Dryads don't need names to know who they are.'

'I envy you,' said This-Way-Up. 'I don't think I'll truly know who I am until I get myself a decent name. If you know any please tell me.'

'The names I know are not the kind that humans give or keep,' the dryad said.

'I'd like to hear them anyway – if you don't mind.'

The wood spirit considered him and his predicament. 'You have an honest face for one of your race. Very well. Unkulunkulu.'

'I beg your pardon?'

'Unkulunkulu. An African god. The name means "very old one".'

'I'm not old,' said This-Way-Up.

'Humbaba then. A nature god. Humbaba has something of Man about him. His face looks like human entrails.'

'Do you have any others?'

'You might consider Huitzilopochtli.'

'I might, if I could pronounce it.'

'Kilibob?' said the dryad. 'Inar? Geb? Awonawilona? Or Leshy, what about Leshy? A god of the forest. I see him sometimes. Human in shape, if a trifle blue in colour, with an eccentric tendency to wear his shoes on the wrong feet.'

This-Way-Up shook his head. 'A name is such a personal thing.'

'Pah!' exclaimed the dryad suddenly.

'I'm sorry,' said This-Way-Up. 'I don't mean to offend you. I know you're trying to help.'

'No, no. Pah is the moon god of the Pawnee, greatly honoured by those people.'

'I'll think it over,' said This-Way-Up.

The dryad drifted away between the trees and This-Way-Up returned to the path that had brought him into the woods. He was some way along it when the dryad's voice came wafting after him.

This-Way-Up left the wood.

After a while he came to a large country house with a neat garden bound by a neat wall. In the garden people chatted and laughed in their best clothes. He was about to pass by when he heard hushed voices on the other side of the wall. He stood on tiptoe to look over. A young man and woman sat there talking quietly. In her arms the woman held a baby, which was sleeping.

'But we must decide,' she was saying with some agitation.

'It's the little one's Naming Day,

the guests all here,

and we can't make up our

minds what to call him!'

'Let's go over them again,' the young father replied, and began listing names. 'Gilbert, Thomas, Frederick, Miles, Fergus, Douglas, Denzil, Bruno, Roger. Any of those?'

'No,' the mother said. 'Let me try. Trevor, Will, Nigel, Abner, Mungo, Andrew, Lucus, Kurt, Tom, Dick, Harry.'

On the off chance that one of their suggestions might suit him too, This-Way-Up listened more closely.

'**Marlon,**' said the father.

'Clive, Walter, Kevin,

Antonio,

Neil,

Josh,

Abraham,

Matthew,

Mark,

Luke...Tom?'

'Ninian,' said the mother. 'Victor, Pierre, Liam, Bernard, Bruce, Alexander, Attila, Caesar, Brutus, Gaius, Caligula, Ptolemy, Fred.'

'Agamemnon,' said the father. 'Ulysses, Achilles, Hector, Paris.'

'Carlo,' said the mother. 'Oliver, George, Ernest, David, Adrian, Reginald.'

'Zachary,' said the father, running out of steam. 'Zeb. Zeke. Zippo.' He cast about in desperation. 'Eric?'

'They're calling us!'
the mother cried.
'It's time!
What shall we do?'

The young parents got to their feet and, cradling their little one between them, walked towards their guests leaning against one another as if going to their execution. But then, quite suddenly, a shiver went through the woman as a new name came to her. She whispered it in the father's ear.

His face lit up and he laughed, and when the moment came to announce the baby's name they beamed at one another and said in one voice:

'We name this child...Jack.'

The guests broke into tumultuous applause, the newly named babe joined in with a scream, and This-Way-Up went on his way.

Some distance on he came upon a wizened little man sitting on a leaguestone at the roadside. This fellow had a lively, cunning look about him, with sly sharp eyes and a wiry grey beard.

'Hail, stranger,' said he. 'Fine day for a stroll.'

'For a stroll perhaps,' returned This-Way-Up. 'But not for finding a name.'

'Have you lost one then?' said the gnome or whatever he was, for the look of him suggested that he was not precisely human.

'I never had one,' answered This-Way-Up. 'And let me tell you, it's no easy matter choosing one when you can take your pick of all. Lucky the child whose name is decided by others, leaving him no choice but to lump it.'

'I could give you a name,' said the other.

'An excellent name,

the very best imaginable.'

'You could?'

'Indeed. Names are my business. I myself have one that many would crave if they but knew it.'

'Oh, what's that then?' enquired the curious lad.

The gnomic little fellow laid a finger alongside his nose. 'I share my name with no one. But what do you say we make ourselves a bargain, young sir?'

'What sort of bargain?'

'I will give you a dozen high-quality, seldom-used names to sift through for no fee at all other than that you guess mine.'

'You want me to guess your name?' said This-Way-Up. 'But how could I? It might be anything.'

'Of course it might,' replied the diminutive chap, 'which is as good as saying it must be something.' A crooked grin broke through the matted grey fastness of his beard and moustache. 'Perhaps you'd be more tempted to take up my challenge if I were to allow you a dozen tries at my name to match the dozen I'll give you if you succeed. Mm?'

'I might. Yes, I might. What have I to lose?'

'Not a thing,' said the little man, if man he was.

This-Way-Up folded his arms over his chest, stared into space, made ready to run through the names he'd heard today and the half-dozen attached to the boys at the orphanage. But as he prepared to pick a few out an odd thing happened.

His mind went quite, quite blank.

'I can't think of a single one,' he said. 'Not so much as an initial.'

'Come, come,' said the gnome. 'One, surely. And one may lead to another, and that to a third, all the way to twelve.'

'Wait,' said the boy. 'I think one's coming. Oh, but it's no sort of name. I have no idea why it's in my head at all. My mind must have been so desperate that it just made one up.'

'Spit it out,' said the dwarf,
already enjoying himself.

'Let's hear it, this ridiculous name that you
think might be mine.'

'Well – all right,' said This-Way-Up, blushing. 'Could it be,' he said haltingly, 'could it be... I'm sorry about this, but the only name I can think of is...'

'Yes?' said the other, jumping up and down excitedly.

'Rumpelstiltskin.'

The dwarf's eyes popped. His hair stood up like wire springs. His beard shot out in several directions at once. He jumped off the leaguestone in a fury.

'How did you know?'

This-Way-Up gaped. 'That's it? I got it right first time?'

'You cheated!'

yelled Rumpelstiltskin.

'You must have!'

'I did not,' the accused retorted indignantly. 'I don't know how to. Cheating wasn't on the curriculum at the orphanage.'

The other was not persuaded. 'You've been listening at keyholes! You've been talking to beautiful maidens who have it in for me!' His mouth twisted in fury. 'You've been accessing my website!'

Now it was This-Way-Up's turn to be angry. He leaned over the bristling dwarf.

'I guessed your name fair and square. We made a bargain, now you must keep your side of it. Give me twelve good names to choose from or I tell everyone that Rumpelstiltskin is not as good as his word!'

A PAIR OF JACKS

The dwarf snarled with rage. 'I'll keep our precious bargain! But that's the last time I play the name game with your kind. You people trick me at every turn.'

He backed away across the field beside the road, and with every three steps supplied a name from the promised dozen.

'Balthazar!' he spat. 'Zachariah!' he yelled. 'Silas!' he bellowed. 'Reynard! Marcus! Tyrone! Ahab! Cormac! Aesop! Jeremiah! Virgil! There! Twelve good names and true, as promised. Choose one and do with the rest as you will!'

'That was only eleven!'

shouted This-Way-Up

at the retreating figure.

'You can't count

"There"!'

Rumpelstiltskin counted on his fingers as he backed the last few steps to the horizon, and realised his mistake. 'Twelve names I said, and twelve names I intended. Here is the twelfth.'

He said the twelfth name, but so far off was he by this time that This-Way-Up wasn't sure he heard right.

'Sorry, what was that?!

Speak up!'

'Jack!' shrieked the distant dwarf.

'Jack! Jack!

Do you hear me now?

JACK!'

This-Way-Up thought for a minute after Rumpelstiltskin dropped below the horizon. Such a long minute did he think that after a while it became two, and pretty soon three, but then he shook himself and looked at the leaguestone, which informed him that the nearest town was V miles distant.

He set off in that direction.

While he walked he tried to recall the names he'd heard that day. Some he would never remember, particularly the ones supplied by the dryad, but most of the others had come back to him by the time he'd gone two or three miles. He mulled over each in turn, testing the sound and weight of them one by one, holding them against him like a row of shirts to see which suited him best – and cast them aside, one after the other, until there were none left.

'So many names and not one that's really me,' he said to himself. 'Why am I so hard to please?'

He leant on a gate and gazed into a field
hoping for inspiration. By the gate wild garlic
grew, Jack-by-the-hedge it was called. A
jackdaw flew down to see if he had anything
worth stealing. A jack rabbit bounded across
the field. Two men strolled by on the road,
one a right jack-a-dandy, the other a jack of
all trades (and a bit of a Jack-the-lad to boot)
whittling a piece of wood with a jackknife.

This-Way-Up pushed himself away
from the gate. No inspiration there!

Reaching the town, he drank deeply from the fountain in the market square. He was hungry too, but the finding of the right name was more important than the pleadings of his stomach. He walked slowly through the town, looking and listening for names, or ideas for names. On the way he passed a group of card players in the shade of an imported jacaranda tree.

One of them held a jack of hearts, a jack of spades, a jack of clubs and a jack of diamonds. When he threw in his hand he collected the jackpot.

A husband and wife were quarrelling in the street.

'Jackass!' screeched the woman. 'Jackanapes! Cheapjack!'

A steeplejack clung to the church spire eating a jacket potato, while down below bowls players aimed at the jack and a builder told his crew that if they didn't work harder every man-jack of them would be out on their ear before they could say Jack Robinson.

This-Way-Up walked out of town, head hung low. Not a hint, not a clue, what was he to do?

He hadn't gone more than half a mile, however, when he pulled up so sharply that he fell over his feet.

'I've got it!' he said, getting up. 'At last!'

And he had.

For in his head, completely out of the blue, sat the name that he knew must be his. The One True Name. A name that suited him utterly and totally and down to the ground. He could only gasp that a name so absolutely right hadn't occurred to him before. This-Way-Up – soon to be This-Way-Up no longer – whooped for joy and clicked his heels in the air.

CLICK

'I'm going to call myself,' he said in breathless triumph, and started again the more to savour the perfect name for him.

'I'm going to call myself... Dick!'

Which is a pity.

Because there's no place in this story

for a Dick.

Please forget you read it.

TALL-TALE JACK

Once upon a time (sorry, but it had to be said) there was a great and powerful lord who owned twelve lakes, several cities, a couple of deserts and a kebab stall. He also had more servants than he could shake a stick at, so he didn't. One of these servants was a young man named… yes, that's right. Jack.

Now Jack's job was to do whatever his master told him to, but if ever he could get out of doing any work he would, and the way he got out of it was by telling whopping great fibs. He would never say, for instance, 'Sorry I'm late, Master, I overslept.' No, he would say something like: 'I was on my way to work just after dawn as usual, Master, when something amazing happened.

This old brass lamp fell off this window ledge and this old genie popped out and said

"Your wish is my command, Jack, and if you don't wish for something I'll die."

Well I couldn't let him die, could I, so I wished for something. I wished that you would live to a very great age, Master, and never have a day's illness or even toothache. But the genie, he said, "No, Jack." He said, "You can't wish for something for someone else, even though it shows what a kind-hearted lad you are, whose master should consider himself lucky to have you.

"No," he said, "you must wish for something for yourself, and be quick about it, I'm on my last legs here."

Well, Master, I thought and thought, and it wasn't easy because there's nothing I want in the whole world except to continue serving you.

But to save the genie I wished that I could spend the morning in bed, and he said "Your wish is my command" and waved his hands, and next thing I knew it was midday,

when I jumped up and rushed here to be at your service by lunchtime, your faithful servant as always.'

To which Jack's long-suffering master could only sigh and tell him to go and clean the windows, or feed the fish, or do anything at all but tell him any more of his tall tales. And Jack would come over all pained and wander off shaking his head, grumbling that no one ever believed the truth these days, what was the world coming to, and so on and so forth.

But one Thursday around teatime, Jack's lord and master decided to find out if there was any more to his servant than met his eye or if he really was that useless.

'Jack,' he said.

'Got a little job for you.'

'Job?' said Jack, just managing not to groan.

'I want you to take a message to one of my cities. Place called Nineveh, just across the desert. Shouldn't take you more than a week there and back by camel.'

'What sort of message?' Jack asked with a sinking heart.

'I want you to tell the citizens of Nineveh that if they don't start paying their taxes on time they'll find themselves on the streets – someone else's.'

'You want me to tell them that?' said Jack in horror.

'Yes, that's what I want you to tell them.'

'But Master, no, seriously, messages aren't my thing. I'm no good with messages, never was, specially ones containing threats.'

'So here's your chance to learn.'

'Master,' Jack wailed, 'send someone else, I beg you. I'll make a mess of it, I guarantee it. And think what could happen. Those people don't know me from Eve. They might kill me the moment I open my trap.'

'That is a possibility,' said the great lord sympathetically.

'So I can stay here?' Jack said hopefully.

'No. You leave first thing in the morning.'

Jack did not leave first thing in the morning; he left that very night, under cover of darkness. He didn't go in the direction his master had told him to either, but the other way entirely, towards the coast. He reached the coast around first light, and there found a cargo vessel about to set sail for Tarshish. He'd never been to Tarshish, knew nothing about Tarshish, but Tarshish had to be better than Nineveh, where he might get thumped, or worse, for giving the citizens that message from his master.

Jack paid the captain of the vessel for his passage to Tarshish and went below.

Quite worn out after rushing through the night, he fell asleep at once.

An hour passed. Then another. Nice voyage so far, but when a bank of heavy cloud rolled out of the west and hovered over the ship, the crew became a little concerned.

But not Jack.
He slept on.

In a while, the wind got up and began to howl around the ship and crack the sails. The crew held onto their hats, definitely worried now.

But not Jack. He slept on.

Then the waves began to heave and leap and toss the ship as though it had no weight at all. The crew were just a gulp short of terror now.

But not Jack.

Oh no.
Jack slept on.

The captain ordered the crew to throw cargo and personal possessions over the side to lighten the load. They did so, but it made no difference. Thunder rolled and lightning struck the decks, and the winds whisked the ship around on top of the waves.

'Now what?' said the crew.

'Pray,' said one; and suddenly this seemed a very good idea.

The sailors were of many different races, from many different countries, regions, provinces and taverns, and each of them had his own god. Fearing for their lives, they fell to their knees and beseeched their various gods to save them.

'There's never a decent god about when you need one,' said the captain. 'You sacrifice to 'em year in, year out, flatter 'em rotten at every meal, and the first time you ask them for a favour they find something more interesting to do.'

'Maybe there's nothing the gods can do!' the first mate shouted above the roar of the thunder, the howl of the wind, the hiss of the waves on the deck. 'Maybe someone brought bad luck on board with him!'

'Well, that's it then!' the captain shouted back. 'We've had it! His bad luck will be the death of us!'

'Not if we find out which of us it is and get rid of him!' the first mate yelled.

'How do we do that?'
the captain bawled.
'We draw straws!
Whoever gets the short
one is obviously unlucky,
so he'll be the one who
brought the storm!'

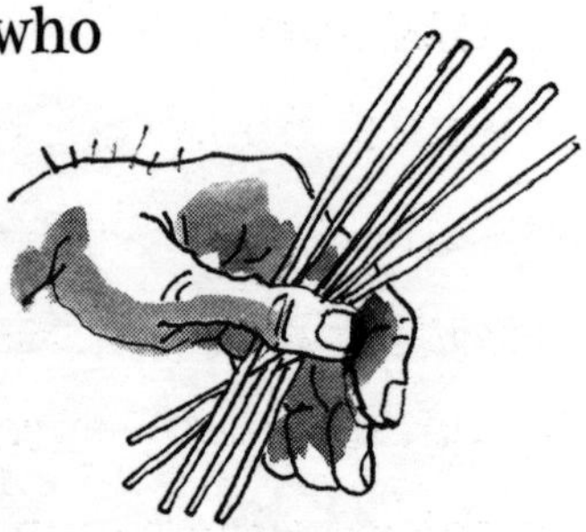

'Brilliant!' the captain hollered. 'Assemble the crew! We'll soon find out who's responsible for this!'

'Don't forget the passenger!' roared the first mate. 'We must test everyone, no exceptions!'

While the crew gathered on deck, the captain went below and shook Jack's shoulder. Jack's eyes flipped open at once. He could sleep through anything except someone shaking his shoulder.

'Master?' he said in bleary panic.

'Captain will do,' said the captain.

'Whew, that's a relief. Are we there?'

'No we're not, and we may never get there unless something's done, and quick. There's a bit of a storm going on up there.'

Just then the ship heaved.

Jack gripped the sides of his bunk. The wind howled. Jack ducked. Lightning struck the keel. Jack whimpered into his hand.

'I'd like you to come up
on deck,' the captain said.

'In this?' Jack replied.
'Are you out of your mind?'

'I'm asking you nicely,'
said the captain, fingering
the knife in his belt.

'Lead the way,'
said Jack.

Up on deck, where the storm raged as furiously as ever if not more so, the men were already taking turns to select straws from the first mate's fist.

'There's just one short straw!' the captain explained to Jack above the roar of the thunder, the howl of the wind, the hiss of the waves. 'The one who draws it is the one who brought bad luck on board!'

'And what happens to him?' asked Jack, who had a bad feeling about this.

'We chuck him over the side to swim for it!' the captain shouted. 'Or drown, whichever he's best at!'

'Your turn!' the first mate bawled, offering his fist to Jack.

Jack snatched a straw.

The short one.

'I knew it was him!' screamed the first mate. 'Once he's gone the storm'll ease off, you see if it don't! Over the side with him!'

'You can't do this!' cried Jack.

'I've paid my fare!'

'I'd give you a refund,' the captain yelled, 'but where would you spend it?'

And over the side went Jack.

Down he went, down and down went he, until his cheeks were like grapefruits and his eyeballs like plums. But then, up he came, up and up, to splutter and gasp and thrash about on the surface. And what did he find there? Well, would you believe it? The thunder and lightning had ceased, the wind no longer howled, the ocean was almost calm, and the ship was sailing away with a cheering crew.

Jack, however, was in no mood to celebrate. Here he was, alone in the middle of the ocean without so much as a boat or plank or paddle, and not a speck of land on any horizon.

But then he saw, coming up behind him at sea level, an enormous fish with its great fat mouth open.

'Oh, lucky day,' said Jack as the big
fish swallowed him in a single gulp.

Into the fish's mouth he
tumbled, head over heels
into a blubbery cave, where
he found himself knee
deep in salt water with
foam on it.

Bobbing about in the gloom were bits and pieces of cargo from the ship he'd just left. Among these oddments were

a wooden kitchen chair,

a jug of ale,

and some formerly dry biscuits.

Jack sat down on the chair, swigged some of the ale, and nibbled a wet dry biscuit. While he was doing this the big fish swallowed a shoal of much smaller fish. In they came, by the thousand, all wide-eyed and silvery, on a mighty wave that sent Jack flying off his chair.

But this was only the beginning.

Fish continued to arrive, in crazy quantities, along with the odd crab and octopus, and shells of all kinds and sizes with startled creatures inside them. There was also an awful lot of seaweed, which was very slimy, especially the bit that slapped him round the face for not paying attention. But worse than that, much worse, was the big fish's habit of belching without warning – a deafening bark that time after time sent Jack crashing against one or another of its teeth with his arms about his head.

Most of the stuff the fish swallowed continued on through its system, and Jack would undoubtedly have gone the same way sooner or later if he hadn't grabbed a passing length of rope and tied himself and his chair to what he imagined must be a tonsil. It certainly looked like a tonsil, being one of a pair and in the right position at the back of the fish's throat.

Now there isn't a lot to do inside a fish, especially when you're tied to a chair and a tonsil, so for three days and three nights Jack just sat there trying to dodge everything that came at him and bemoaning his fate.

It wasn't fair.

All he'd ever wanted was a quiet life with his feet up. If that bullying ex-master of his hadn't given him such a difficult task he'd be at home this minute doing what he was best at, which was nothing.

Towards the dawn
of the third night of
his ordeal, Jack saw,
through the fish's
open mouth...

'Land!'

He might have got very excited about this, but just then he heard a great noise like an earthquake and a hurricane and an erupting volcano all rolled into one, and it was coming from behind him, where all the little fishes and crabs and octopuses and seaweed and shells had gone. Something the big fish had eaten had not agreed with it and it was coming back up, along with everything else down there.

'Oh no!' cried Jack as a great, thick, horrible, stinking tide of nastiness rolled and gurgled towards him.

On it came, on and on, and soon the whole roaring fishload of disgustingness was coursing about him like a dark wave dotted with rubbish. Then the rope that tied Jack to the chair and the chair to the tonsil pulled apart, and he was catapulted into the tide of ghastly muck, which carried him out of the giant fish's mouth and into shallow salt water.

Jack lay in the indescribable mess with his bottom in the air.

He rolled over.

Schloop.

He sat up in the vile mush.

Schlup.

He clawed goo from his eyes and peered about him. 'Oh,' he said, as well he might. For the sun had risen, the sky was blue, the air was fresh, and best of all the big fish, having emptied its stomach all over the shore (and him with it), was heading back to the deepest ocean to find something else to snack on.

But almost at once Jack found two tiny blips in his happiness. The first was that he knew this shore. It was the one he'd left a few nights ago. The other was the man standing at the edge of it, peering at him.

'What happened here?' said his lord and master, for it was he.

Jack spat out a small crab. 'It's kind of complicated,' he said, in a heavily disguised voice.

'I can't wait to hear about it,' said the other.

So, believing his face to be pretty well concealed by the contents of the fish's belly, Jack began his story.

'Well, I was on this ship, see, minding my own business, when this terrible storm struck up and the crew drew straws to see whose fault it was and I got the short one and they slung me over the side. Then this fish as big as a house came along and swallowed me, and I lived inside it for three days and nights, tied to a chair and a tonsil, and...

...what are you looking at me like that for?'

'Sorry, it's just that you remind me of someone. What's your name?'

'Oh, my name's J...' Jack stopped. He was talking to the one person in the world he dare not give his real name to.

'Is that it?' the great lord asked. 'J?'

'No, no,' said Jack, 'that would be plain silly, wouldn't it?'

'It would rather,' the great lord agreed.

Jack cast about for another name starting with J. One came to him. 'Jonah,' he said.

'What?' said the great lord.

'The J. That's what it stands for. Jonah.'

'Oh, I see. Well, as you remind me so much of someone I used to think very highly of, why don't you let me treat you to a bath and a hearty breakfast?'

Jack knew his lord and master well. He knew that he wasn't easily fooled, and that he wasn't fooled now. All he could do was try and make the best of a tricky situation.

He struggled to his feet.

Sshlooop!

'Oh no, thanks, but I can't stop, I've got a job to do and I'm running late.'

'What job's that, if I may ask?' said the great lord.

'I have to go to this place called Nineveh and give the people an important message,' Jack said.

His master smiled.

'Good lad,' he said.

So Jack went to Nineveh after all. On the way he told his tale to everyone he met: how he'd been cast overboard in a terrible storm and lived for three days and nights inside a big fish that had eventually thrown him up at the feet of his master (who, after a telling or two, became the most powerful master anyone could imagine). And do you know, people actually believed him!

Well, most of them did.

I didn't when he told me.

Not a word.

Do you?

A PAIR OF JACKS

All priced at £4.99

The Jack stories are available from all good bookshops,
or can be ordered direct from the publisher:
Orchard Books, PO BOX 29, Douglas IM99 1BQ
Credit card orders please telephone 01624 836000
or fax 01624 837033 or visit our internet site: www.orchardbooks.co.uk
or e-mail: bookshop@enterprise.net for details.

To order please quote title, author and ISBN
and your full name and address.
Cheques and postal orders should be made payable to 'Bookpost plc.'
Postage and packing is FREE within the UK
(overseas customers should add £2.00 per book).

Prices and availability are subject to change.